Good Night, Lewis!

A Random House PICTUREBACK®

In memory of my father,

Samuel J. Margolin

—H.M.Z.

Library of Congress Cataloging in Publication Data: Ziefert, Harriet. Good night, Lewis! SUMMARY: Mama finally figures out that Lewis doesn't like to go to bed because he's afraid in the dark. [1. Bedtime—Fiction. 2. Fear—Fiction. 3. Night—Fiction] I. Nicklaus, Carol. II. Title.   PZ7.Z487Go 1986   [E]   85-14306   ISBN: 0-394-87617-2 (trade); 0-394-97617-7 (lib. bdg.)
Manufactured in the United States of America   3 4 5 6 7 8 9 0

Good Night, Lewis!

by Harriet Ziefert and Carol Nicklaus

RANDOM HOUSE NEW YORK

Lewis took a bath all by himself, then put on his pajamas.

Mama came to help Lewis button his pajamas. She said, "Stop wriggling, Lewis. I'll never get your bottoms buttoned."

Mama left the bathroom. She knew Lewis could brush his teeth by himself.

Soon Mama called from downstairs, "Lewis, are you almost finished?"
"Almost, Mama," Lewis answered. Then he started to draw another
squiggle picture in the sink.

When Mama came back, she didn't want to look at Lewis's pictures. She said, "Now it's time for bed."

"But I'm not ready!" Lewis said.

Mama didn't seem to hear. She walked Lewis to his bedroom and took a book from the shelf.

"I need to feed my fish," Lewis said. "And I need to say good night to my turtle...and I need to fix my rocking horse."

Mama was tired of waiting for Lewis. She said, "I need you to get into your bed so we can read a bedtime story."

Mama and Lewis read the whole book.

Then Mama gave Lewis a quick kiss and said, "Now I'm turning off your light. It's time for you to go to sleep."

Lewis said, "Please don't turn my light off yet. I want to read by myself."

"All right," Mama said. "You can read one story by yourself."

In a little while Mama called, "Lewis, time to turn off your light."

Lewis didn't want his light OFF.
He wanted his light ON.

Mama marched into Lewis's room. She said, "Good night. Sleep tight. I'm turning off your light."

"But I want to read another story," Lewis said.

"No more stories," Mama answered. "Here's Dubby. Good night. Sleep tight. I'm turning off your light."

"I think I have to go to the bathroom," Lewis said.

"You just went to the bathroom," Mama reminded Lewis. "Good night. Sleep tight. I'm turning off your light."

"What if I wake up in the middle of the night and it's all dark and I can't find the light and I wet my pajamas?"

"I really don't think that will happen," Mama said.

"Wait, Mom!" Lewis shouted. "I think I heard a funny noise. I really did. I know I did. Dubby heard it too. Maybe there's a noisy monster under my bed."

"Lewis, there are no monsters under your bed! Good night. Sleep tight. I'm definitely turning off your light."

Mama clicked off the light and left the room.
Lewis was all alone in the dark.

Lewis looked around his room. It looked different.
Lewis began shaking all over. He tried to stop but he couldn't.

Lewis tried hiding under the covers.

"MAMA!" Lewis yelled.

"What's the matter?" Mama asked.

Lewis didn't say anything. Finally he answered, "I want you to stay with me until I go to sleep."

"Why?" Mama asked.

"I feel scared," Lewis said. "I'm scared of the dark."

"What's scary?" Mama asked.

"My fish tank...my clothes tree...my rocking horse...they look scary when my room is all dark. They look like monsters and dragons and mean things."

Now Mama understood why Lewis was afraid.

Mama had a good idea. "Lewis," she said, "I think there is something in the attic that will make you feel better."

"What is it?" Lewis asked.

"It's a night light," Mama answered. "Would you like to help me find it?"

"Why will a night light make me feel better?" Lewis asked.

"Because when you go to sleep, it will keep shining," Mama explained. "If you happen to wake up, you'll be able to see its glow."

Mama plugged the night light right next to Lewis's bed.

Then she said, "Good night. Sleep tight. I'm leaving on your night light."

"Can I have a kiss?" Lewis asked.

"You can have two kisses—one for you and one for Dubby," Mama answered.

Now Lewis was ready to go to sleep.
He whispered to Dubby, "All right. Night light. Sleep tight. Good night."

Good night, Lewis.